DANCE TEAM
DRAMA

BY JAKE MADDOX

text by
Leigh McDonald

STONE ARCH BOOKS
a capstone imprint

Jake Maddox JV Girls books are published by
Stone Arch Books
a Capstone imprint
1710 Roe Crest Drive
North Mankato, Minnesota 56003

www.mycapstone.com

Library of Congress Cataloging-in-Publication Data is available on the Library of
Congress website.

ISBN: 978-1-4965-3674-7 (library binding)
ISBN: 978-1-4965-3678-5 (paperback)
ISBN: 978-1-4965-3682-2 (ebook PDF)

Summary: Lily Richter is forced to leave behind both her best friend and her middle school
dance team when her family moves at the beginning of the school year. Faced with an
unfamiliar school, new teammates, and a team captain who seems to have it out for her, Lily
struggles to dance her best.

Art Director: Nathan Gassman
Designer: Kayla Rossow
Media Researcher: Morgan Walters
Production Specialist: Tori Abraham

Photo Credits:
Shutterstock: Aaron Amat, (basketball) 96, Angie Makes, design element, cluckva, design
element, Dan Kosmayer, (stick) 96, Eky Studio, design element, irin-k, (soccer ball) 96,
Lightspring, (volleyball) 96, Lorraine Swanson, Cover, Markus Gann, design element,
SFIO CRACHO, Cover

Printed in the United States of America in Stevens Point, Wisconsin.
009622F16

TABLE OF CONTENTS

CHAPTER 1

DANCE CAMP

Lily Richter's hands hit the floor. She pushed and launched herself back onto her feet in a perfect back handspring. Her arms snapped straight up to finish the move and then out to her sides as she lunged forward. She spun into a graceful pirouette, followed by another. Then it was back to second position stance.

Without even looking, Lily knew she was in perfect step with her best friend Amy, who danced beside her. Their bodies moved confidently in time with the loud, pumping music.

Hips swaying and shoulders dipping, Lily jazz-walked forward. After seven steps, she stepped to the side and crossed her working foot over her supporting foot. Then she pivoted quickly and took four cross steps to the left.

With a bright smile, Lily thrust her arms out to the sides like a T. She knew that Amy had stepped into place right behind her. Stiffening her body, Lily fell straight back.

Amy caught her teammate smoothly. With their arms linked for support, Lily rolled across her friend's raised knee with a high double kick.

Perfect, thought Lily as she landed back on the floor.

The two girls marched off in opposite directions to form a circle with the rest of their dance team. Several of the dancers broke into the center, causing the circle to bend into a star formation.

As the last notes of the song blasted out, Lily snapped her hands up high. She stood triumphantly in line with four of her teammates. Amy and the other girls had dropped into a dramatic floor pose in front of them. It was the perfect flourish to end the routine.

Coach Jackson applauded loudly. "Very nice, ladies!" she exclaimed.

Lily felt as triumphant as she looked. Dance camp was always her favorite time of year. It was a time to bond with her teammates, have fun, and get her mind and body in shape for the long dance season — and school year — to come.

This year was even better than most. Lily had her best friend by her side, new dance skills to show off, and a wonderful coach to learn from. Now they were only a week away from the beginning of eighth grade. She felt completely ready to take on the new year and the new season.

The girls broke out of formation. Everyone jumped around happily. Amy linked her arm through Lily's with a big grin.

"You were awesome!" Amy gushed. "That handspring was perfect!"

"You were amazing too!" Lily replied. She sighed happily. "Dance is the best."

She and Amy had been taking lessons with a private dance school for years. In sixth grade, they had both joined the Greenville Middle School dance team. Dance was Lily's life, and she loved being able to share that passion with teammates.

"Good work this morning, team," Coach said. "Let's go ahead and break for lunch. I have some announcements to share at the end of the meal."

The girls ran off to the bunk rooms to wash up and change before the meal. Dance was fun, but it was also a lot of work! Everyone was sweaty and exhausted after a whole morning on the floor. Now, they were also really hungry.

After getting cleaned up, Lily and her friend Kala ran down the stairs. They were the first ones to arrive in the kitchen at the camp house. The two girls started carrying the trays of sandwiches, salads, and drinks out to the buffet tables in the dining hall.

By the time everything was ready, the other girls had formed a line. Lily and Kala each grabbed a plate and joined in. After getting their food, they found a seat at one of the long tables.

"What do you think Coach is going to say?" a tall girl named Dani asked, taking a large bite of her turkey sandwich.

Lily shrugged. "I don't know, maybe hand out practice schedules and stuff? Actually, I haven't even gotten my class schedule yet, have you?"

"No," Dani replied. "I'm really hoping I have Mrs. Kraft for English, though . . ."

Amy plopped down next to Lily with her plate of food. "We'd better have the same lunch period, at least!" she said.

Happy chatter filled the room as the dance team ate and relaxed. Julia, who had brought her guitar, ate quickly and then began playing some music.

Just as everyone was finishing their food, Coach Jackson walked in and clapped her hands to get the team's attention. The team quieted down. Lily turned around to hear what their coach had to say.

"As you all know, school starts in a week. Practices begin that Tuesday — I'm passing out the schedule now." She handed some papers to Julia. "Our first performance will be at a school pep rally in four weeks. We'll need to hit the ground running to get our act together in time."

The girls at Lily's table exchanged excited smiles. Everyone was looking forward to the first performance.

"That's not all," Coach said. "I have one more important piece of news to share — the name of our team captain!"

Lily nervously gulped down the rest of the cookie she had been nibbling. Being team captain of the Greenville Lions was all she'd ever dreamed about. Would this be the year?

Amy nudged Lily and gave her hand a tight squeeze. "You've got this," Amy whispered.

"I'm so pleased to announce that due to her teamwork, spirit, and excellence on the floor," Coach continued, "the Lions' team captain for this year will be . . . Lily Richter!"

Lily gasped as happy tears sprang to her eyes. All the girls in the room started clapping and cheering.

"Told you so!" Amy said with a laugh.

Lily jumped up and threw her arms around her best friend. Soon the whole team was surrounding her in a giant group hug.

Team captain! thought Lily, still a little dazed. *Now I* know *this is going to be the best year yet.*

CHAPTER 2

BIG NEWS

That afternoon, Lily spotted her mom's car pulling into the parking lot. She jumped up from the steps of the camp house and raced to the curb. Her suitcase bounced along behind her.

"Bye, Dani! Bye, Kala! See you next week!" she called over her shoulder. Only a handful of girls were still waiting for their rides home from camp.

Lily's mother got out and gave her daughter a big hug. "Hey, sweetie!" she said.

"Hi, Mom! You'll never guess my great news!" Lily began happily.

Mom smiled, but there was an odd look in her eyes.

"Oh?" she said, taking Lily's suitcase and lifting it into the trunk. "Let's get in the car, and you can share. I have some news too."

They climbed in the car. Lily waved once more to her friends as they pulled away. Then she turned to face her mom.

"So camp was fun?" Mom asked.

"Yes! And the best part is, Coach made me team captain!" Lily burst out. Her excitement was too big to contain.

"That's great, Lily. I'm so proud of you," Mom said. Then she took a deep breath. "But remember how I said I had some news too?"

"Yes . . ." Lily said. Her excitement began to fade and worry settled in its place. Her mom was acting strange. She knew how much Lily had wanted to be team captain, but now she was barely acting happy about the news.

"Well, while you were at camp, I got a promotion too!" Mom said, smiling. It was a nervous smile.

Lily's worried feeling grew. *Why would Mom be nervous about a promotion?*

"That's so great, Mom," she said. "Congrats!"

"Yes, I'm going to be a regional manager now. It's a big step up. I've been working hard for years to get this position," Mom explained. "But . . . it's in Wilmington."

Lily blinked. "Wait, you're moving to Wilmington?" she asked, confused. "That's, like, four hours away! You can't live four hours away."

"No, honey," her mom said. "*We* are moving to Wilmington. Our family. You and I head out on Friday." Mom didn't look at Lily but kept her eyes locked on the road.

"What . . . Friday? That's in five days," Lily said. The news still wasn't sinking in.

"Dad will stay to pack up the house, and then he'll join us later. We'll be there just in time for the first day of school."

Lily's mind was racing. *Moving? Now? Right before school starts?* She could hear that her mom was still talking, but she couldn't listen anymore. A new school, new kids she didn't know, and . . .

"Mom! What about dance team?" Lily burst out. "I can't leave my team! I can't go into eighth grade with no dance team!" Tears suddenly sprang to her eyes.

"Don't worry! I called and talked to the Wilmington dance coach," Mom assured her. "They have a great team, and you've only missed camp. You can still join. All you have to do is a quick special tryout to show them you're as good as I said you are. Don't worry, honey, I know how important dance is to you!"

Lily didn't say anything. She just stared out the window as tears ran down her cheeks, watching the trees and houses rolling by. This wasn't her home anymore. She wasn't going to be team captain or enter eighth grade as a dance team champion with her best friends by her side. She was moving.

"I know this is sudden," Mom said. "I'm really sorry about that. But . . . at least you'll get to start fresh with the new school year, right?"

Lily sniffed and blinked back tears. She nodded a little, then took a deep breath. "I need to call Amy," she finally managed to say.

* * *

"Moving?" Amy shouted over the phone. "You can't be serious!"

"I know!" Lily said, flopping back on her bed. She and her mom had just gotten home, but half-filled boxes were already lurking in the corners of the room. She had only been at camp for a week, and everything had changed.

"But you're team captain! You can't leave!" Amy wailed.

Lily sighed. "Well, maybe Coach will make you captain now. You deserve it. Silver lining?"

"I don't want a silver lining, I want my best friend!" Amy said angrily. She took a deep breath. "If there's really nothing we can do to stop this from happening, I have to help you put together a killer routine for your tryout. No way are you moving *and* missing out on dance team. See if your mom will let me come over for dinner."

* * *

Later that evening, after eating lots of pizza, the two friends huddled around Lily's laptop in her room. They were watching dance videos on YouTube and writing down ideas for the tryout routine.

Since Lily didn't have much time, Amy had suggested she use the same song and basic routine they'd been working on at camp. Now all they needed to do was change a few things for it to work as a solo.

"Oh, see that rolling move she does there?" Lily said, pausing the video. She backed it up and hit play. "I could do that in place of the kick."

"Yeah," Amy agreed. "That would be great. And then go straight into the walk. But what about the formation? You need something else there too. You can't make a star with one person."

"Ugh," Lily said. "You're right. This is so hard."

"No, you can do it," Amy assured her. "You're going to be awesome. Those Wilmington kids had better know how lucky they are to be getting Lily Richter!"

Lily plopped her head on Amy's shoulder and sighed. "I just hope I can be half as awesome without you."

CHAPTER 3

THE FIRST DAY

The following week, Lily stared out the window of her mom's car. Wilmington Central Junior High was much bigger than Greenville Middle School. Her new school was a large, two-story brick building. Unfamiliar kids streamed up a short flight of steps and disappeared through the wide open doors.

"Well, this is it," Mom said finally, giving Lily's knee a squeeze. "Do you know where you're headed?"

"Yes, Mom," Lily replied, waving a stack of papers. "B102. I've got it." She took a deep breath, then opened the door and stepped out into the bright September sunshine.

"I'll be right here at three thirty!" Mom called as she pulled away.

When the car was gone, Lily joined the crowd and headed up the steps into her new school. Inside, kids were busy greeting friends, studying schedules, and searching for their lockers. Nobody paid attention to the new girl standing in the middle of the hallway, looking lost.

All of a sudden, something heavy knocked Lily forward. Surprised, she turned and saw a tall girl glaring at her.

The girl hiked a large backpack onto her shoulder. "Move, weirdo. People are trying to walk here," she said rudely. Then she spun back to her friends, muttering something.

Lily couldn't hear what the girl had said. She did hear the nasty giggles afterward, though. *Well, I'm off to a great start,* she thought, rolling her eyes.

Lily looked at her schedule again. Her first class was English, with someone named Broadman, in classroom B102. She found the room by following signs on the wall. Taking a seat by the window, she watched as her new classmates slowly filed in.

A girl sat next to her, but before Lily could say anything, she turned to chat with a friend on her other side. A boy wearing headphones plopped down in the seat in front of her and started doodling on his notebook. Finally, Lily just looked out the window and waited for class to begin.

After a few minutes, an older man in a brown suit came in, shutting the door behind him. The loud chatter in the classroom stopped as he began writing on the board.

"I'm Mr. Broadman, and this is eighth grade English," he began. "Let's start with the basics.

When I call your name, please stand up and move to the desk I indicate."

There were groans from around the room.

"Yes, we're doing assigned seats. All right, first up is Aikman, Madison," he said, pointing to a desk in the front of the room. "Anderson, Michael. Beech, Emily."

Kids began to shuffle around the room as names were called. Lily was directed to a seat in the second row, near the middle. The space to her right stayed empty as almost all the other names were called.

"Zabroski, Mia," the teacher said finally, pointing to the seat next to Lily.

A girl from the back of the room sighed loudly as she stomped forward and flopped down in the chair. Lily glanced over and realized with horror that it was the rude girl from the hallway. She looked down quickly before she caught Mia's eye.

The one person Lily had hoped never to see again was now sitting next to her for the rest of the year.

* * *

After quietly suffering through math, history, and P.E., Lily found her way to the cafeteria that afternoon. Her mom had packed a lunch for her, so she didn't need to join the line. She paused inside the doors for a moment, searching for a place to sit.

All the tables had at least a couple of kids sitting at them already. Everyone was chatting happily, and the thought of approaching any of the tables filled her with dread. Then she noticed some open doors on the other side of the room. It looked like they led to a small courtyard area outside.

Maybe I can find a place to sit out there that won't make me feel completely awkward, Lily thought.

She quickly walked outside. There was a small group on the grass, a few couples, and three kids kicking a tiny ball around under a huge tree.

Lily sat on a low wall in the shade and took out her sandwich. She watched the three kids as she ate. One of them, a tall boy with big curly hair, finally glanced over and noticed her watching.

"Hey, you wanna try it?" he offered, flicking the ball over to one of the girls.

Lily jumped a little, surprised. "Oh, me? No!" Then she realized that might have sounded rude and added, "Um, thanks, I mean. It looks fun, but I don't know how to do that. What is it?"

"Really? A hacky sack," the boy said.

"So what *do* you know how to do?" asked the girl. She flipped the hacky sack expertly on to the top of her bright blue sneaker, then bounced it over to her other friend.

"Dance," Lily said. "I'm on the dance team. Or . . . I was at my old school. I'm hoping to join the team here, but I haven't tried out yet."

"Oh!" the girl said. She looked up at Lily and smiled. "I'm on the team. I heard someone new might be coming. What's your name?"

"Lily. I'm from Greenville," she added.

"Jill," the other girl said. "I've been in dance for a while, but this is my first year on a team. It's pretty fun so far. We had camp, but practice doesn't start until tomorrow."

Just then the tall boy kicked the hacky sack back to Jill, and she went back to concentrating on their game. Lily quietly watched them until all her food was gone. She crumpled up the bag and stood.

"Guess I'll see you tomorrow?" Jill called without looking up.

"Yeah, I guess so," Lily said. "Nice to meet you."

"Later," Jill said.

Well, at least that's something *good I can tell Amy about today,* Lily thought as she walked back inside. The whole day had felt like one long disaster, but meeting someone from the team was at least a start.

CHAPTER 4

DANCING SOLO

The next afternoon, Lily walked out of the locker room and into the school gym. Her hands were sweating, and she could feel her heart beating loudly.

The team's first practice wasn't scheduled to begin for another half an hour, but the coach had asked her to come early for a special tryout. She wanted to make sure that Lily was a good fit for the team.

After an hour-long phone call with Amy, Lily had spent the rest of the night before practicing her tryout routine. She'd practiced so much that she'd actually dreamed about it.

She took a deep breath and tried to bring back the confidence she'd always felt dancing with her old teammates. *It's the same moves, just in a different place,* she tried to assure herself.

Lily headed toward the two people sitting on the bleachers. One was a woman wearing a red warm-up jacket and holding a laptop and a bunch of papers. She looked up and smiled as Lily approached, standing to greet her.

As Lily smiled back, she glanced over at the other person — it was Mia!

Lily felt her face go white. But she shook the coach's hand and tried to hide her nervousness. "Hi, I'm Lily," she managed to say.

"Hi, Lily, I'm Coach Smith, and this is our team captain, Mia Zabroski," the coach said.

"Good luck," Mia said, smiling as she stood and shook Lily's hand.

To Lily, the girl's smile looked icy. *This is who's going to be judging me?* she wondered, trying to keep calm.

"I'm sure you don't need luck. I spoke with your old coach, Ms. Jackson," Coach Smith said. "She had great things to say about you. I'm sorry you won't get to be team captain, but there's always next year, right?"

Lily glanced at Mia. Her smile looked even more forced at the mention of Lily possibly being captain. Lily quickly looked away before she lost her nerve. "I guess so," she replied softly.

"Well, we'd better get going," Coach said, gesturing toward the laptop. "Pull your song up, and start whenever you're ready."

Lily nodded and walked over to the computer. It was already set up on a music site. She found her song and took the floor.

Music suddenly filled the room, flooding Lily with a familiar burst of energy. The bass thumped, and she began moving through the routine she knew so well. She finally felt her nerves begin to melt away.

Cambre, cambre, box step. The beginning of the routine was the same as the one Lily had done with the Greenville team. *Kick, ronde de jamb, pivot, kick.*

It seemed like only moments had passed before it was time for the back handspring. The move was one of Lily's favorite parts of the dance, although it was also one of the most challenging.

Lily sprang backward. Her hands hit the floor squarely with her elbows straight, and then she launched herself back to her feet in one smooth motion. She could see Coach Smith and Mia nodding and whispering to each other on the bleachers.

Stay focused, Lily thought. She couldn't worry about them if she wanted to nail her performance.

Spinning into the pirouette, Lily concentrated on her next move. Since she was by herself, she wouldn't be falling backward into Amy's arms. She was moving into the new part of her routine.

Thankfully her practice had paid off, and Lily's body easily went into the different steps. She spun gracefully to the left in a series of short quick turns, called a *chaîné*. Arching her upper body backward, she kicked one leg out in a dramatic jazz layout. As her leg came down, she went into a soft collapse to the floor.

Swinging her legs quickly in front of her body, Lily folded them into a pretzel and rolled slowly up to her feet. A gliding triple step took her across the floor, then she whipped her leg up for a fan kick.

Before Lily knew it, she was jazz walking forward into the sassy final pose. She placed her hand on her hip and confidently thrust her other arm up in the air just as the song ended. Mia and the coach both clapped.

"Well, I can see we won't have any problems adding you to the team!" the coach said, smiling.

"Your movements are crisp and strong, and you have great energy. Wonderful job, Lily."

"Thanks," Lily said, a little breathless. "I love dance — thank you so much for making room for me."

"Even though you're new to the school, I think you'll be a great help in showing our new girls the dance-team ropes. Don't you think, Mia?" Coach added.

Mia shrugged. "Yeah," she replied, sounding bored. "We do have a lot of new girls on the team this year."

Suddenly a door closed in the back of the gym. They all turned. Three girls, all dressed in their workout clothes, had come in through the locker room. Lily recognized one of them as Jill, the girl she'd met in the courtyard.

"That was amazing!" Jill said as the girls walked over. "I hope you don't mind us watching, but we heard the music . . ."

Lily wasn't sure if the flush she felt was from dancing or from all her nerves suddenly returning. She managed a smile anyway. At least Jill was a friendly face. "No, it's fine," she said. "Guess I get to be your teammate."

"Yay!" Jill exclaimed.

"Hello, girls," Coach Smith said. "Go ahead and start with individual stretching and warm-ups while we wait for the others to arrive."

Over the next few minutes, more girls trickled into the gym. Everyone chatted as they began to run through stretches. Lily could tell the dancers had already gotten to know each other really well at camp — just like she had done with the Lions.

At that thought, the small thrill she'd gotten from her tryout success and Jill's warm greeting faded. It was replaced instead by homesickness.

The Lions are probably just starting their first practice too, Lily remembered. *I wish I could be in Greenville with them instead of being stuck here.*

She looked around the room at her new teammates. Jill and the two girls she'd arrived with were running through a series of yoga poses. Other girls had paired off to jog around the gym or do mirror stretches.

Soon Lily found herself standing alone on the sidelines. She might not have been the newest to dancing, but she definitely felt like the odd one out.

Lily turned her back to the other girls and began stretching by herself, even though she was already warmed up from her tryout performance. It looked like Jill and everyone already had their groups — she didn't want to bother anyone by barging in.

Finally the coach clapped her hands. "Over here, everyone," she called.

The girls quickly gathered around. Lily hung back at the edge of the group.

"I have an exciting announcement to make," Coach said, beckoning Lily forward. She put an arm around her shoulders. "This is Lily Richter, joining us from Greenville Middle School. She was just named captain on her old squad, which she unfortunately had to leave. But I think she's going to make a great addition to the Wilmington Panthers. Please make her feel welcome."

The team clapped politely. A few girls called out, "Welcome, Lily!"

Lily tried to smile at them, but she just felt awkward. She gave a small wave then stared at the floor.

"Okay," Coach said, "now that we're all here, let's get this season officially started!"

As the other dancers cheered, Lily frowned. She couldn't work up any excitement for dancing with a team of strangers.

CHAPTER 5

OUT OF SYNC

As they broke from their circle, the girls rushed to set up the floor mats for practice. Lily trailed behind. The team ran through a few more stretches, and then Coach Smith announced that it was time for tumbling practice.

"Each practice, we'll spend time working on a different set of skills you'll need to bring to our dances," Coach explained. "Dance team routines draw from lots of different styles, including jazz, ballet, hip-hop, modern dance, gymnastics, and more. So we have plenty to go over. Today we'll work on gymnastics skills. Everyone take a spot on the mats. Give yourselves some room."

Lily blew out a relieved breath. *At least this will be familiar*, she thought.

On the Lions, she had been one of the most advanced tumblers. Not only had she taken lots of gymnastics classes, but she and Amy had spent hours practicing in Lily's old backyard.

Lily closed her eyes and swallowed a lump in her throat as she felt memories flooding back. *Don't think about that now.*

After reviewing basic moves like rolls and handstands, Coach divided them up to work on handspring skills. By a show of hands, about half of the girls were comfortable with kickovers and limbers. Only Lily and Mia were skilled with both front and back handsprings, though.

"Lily and Mia, I'd like you to work on kickovers and limbers with those who want more practice. Make sure to use proper form," Coach Smith reminded them. "The rest of you will stay here with me to work on handsprings."

Mia nodded confidently and walked over to the far end of the mats. Several girls trailed obediently behind her. Lily followed slowly, at a distance.

"Okay, girls, first the backbend kickover. Start by getting into a bridge," Mia directed.

The team captain lay flat on the mat with her arms above her head. Then she drew in her knees, bending them at a ninety-degree angle. Mia did the same with her arms and put her hands right next to her ears. Raising her hip off the ground and pushing through her legs, she formed a high arch with her body.

"Then you're ready for the kickover," Mia continued.

Pointing her right foot straight out, she easily kicked her leg up. The left leg followed over until she had come out of the bridge and landed on her feet in a lunge position.

Mia turned to the girls. "Be sure to keep your arms straight and up by your ears. But really, it's totally easy."

The dancers all spread out and began working on the skill. Some of them had strong kickovers already, but three were struggling to get their legs up. One fell flat on her back with a heavy *thump*. Mia heaved a disgusted sigh.

Lily stepped forward. "Don't worry," she said, helping the girl back to her feet. "This requires a lot of shoulder strength. When I was learning kickovers, I started with a lot of rocking backbends."

"What's that?" the girl asked.

"Okay, so when you're in the bridge, rock back and forth. Push your shoulders so they go past your hands," Lily instructed. "Once you're comfortable, you can start to hop your feet up a little as you rock back. Don't worry about getting your legs over yet. Just get your shoulders used to the motion."

Lily bent backward into an arch and rocked back and forth several times. Then she started hopping her feet up about a foot off the mat.

"Oh, wow. That seems really helpful," the girl said, looking relieved. She got into a bridge and started rocking. Soon all three girls who had been struggling were practicing the rocking backbend.

Mia gave Lily a long look. "You seem to have this under control," she said. "We'll be working on *actual* kickovers over here." She flipped her hair and stalked off to another mat. The other girls followed behind her.

"Don't worry," one of the girls in Lily's group piped up. "She's always like that."

Lily sighed. "Great."

* * *

After another fifteen minutes of skill practice and a water break, the coach called for everyone to put the mats away and meet back in the middle of the gym floor.

"When I call your name, line up in two rows in front of me. Leave enough space so you can swing your arms without bumping into each other," Coach instructed. "Emily . . . Hannah . . . Lily . . . Alison . . ."

Lily trotted into place next to the girl she figured must be Hannah. She nervously crossed her arms tight while the other girls lined up.

"Hi, Lily," Hannah said with a smile. "Welcome to the team! Are you excited for your first performance with the Panthers at the pep rally? Two weeks isn't a lot of time to get ready, but pep rallies are usually pretty low-pressure performances. It's still totally fun, though."

"Uh, yeah. Sure," replied Lily distractedly. She didn't feel like making small talk with anyone right now. Practice so far had felt weird and unfamiliar with the new team, plus Mia was being rude every chance she got.

All I want is to go home — my real home in Greenville, Lily thought. She turned back toward the front without saying another word to Hannah.

Hannah looked a little confused and like she was about to say something else. But then she just gave a small sigh and turned to talk to Emily instead. Lily stood silently with her arms crossed until all the girls had formed two loose rows, standing several feet apart.

"Great. We'll be practicing staying in sync," Coach told them. "I'm going to start the music, and I want one pair to jump on each beat, like a wave. Just listen to the rhythm for the first eight-count. We'll start jumping on the second eight. Okay?"

The team nodded. Lily shook out her arms. She just needed to get through the rest of practice.

"Clap above your head as you land, and keep your arms up," the coach continued. "We'll start with Emily and Nora on this end and go down the line."

The dancers were ready to go, so Coach Smith pushed a button on her laptop. Music began blaring from the speakers.

Lily bopped her head for the first eight beats. Emily and Nora jumped and clapped on the start of the second eight-count. Waiting for her turn, Lily sprang up on cue. Down the line, each pair jumped with the beat.

Coach paused the music. "Pretty good for a first try. Lily and Alison, you were a little late," she noted.

Lily frowned. *Late? But it was just a simple pairs jump!*

"Let's try it again," Coach said. "This time, when we get to the end of the row, keep it going back the other way. Bring your arms down when the beat comes back to you. Here we go."

The music played for several bars as the girls took turns jumping. Lily waited for the rhythm to take over like it usually did when she was dancing. But after being called out, she felt self-conscious in front of all the unfamiliar faces. Was she still late? Early?

Lily tried to block the distractions and just focus on the beat. But the more she focused on matching her body with the music, the worse it got. It almost felt as if her feet belonged to someone else.

I can't do this! Lily thought helplessly as she landed behind the beat again. She saw the coach frown slightly. *I don't want to be a Wilmington Panther. I want my Greenville Lions!*

CHAPTER 6

MOVING ON

"Save me, Amy!" Lily whined into the phone after school.

She had been in Wilmington for almost two weeks now. But instead of feeling better about her new town and school, she was feeling worse and worse. She'd thought joining dance team would help her feel at home. But it was just making her miss her old team even more.

"Uh-oh," Amy said, sighing. "It's still that bad? But what about your room? Is it cool now that you have your stuff?"

Lily flopped back onto her bed. The walls were still bare. Aside from her clothes, most of her stuff was still stuffed in boxes scattered around the room. Her dad and their belongings had finally arrived a week ago, but she hadn't been very interested in making this house feel like a home.

"Actually, I haven't set anything up yet," Lily admitted.

"Lily, it's been a week!" Amy said.

"I know, I just . . . haven't gotten around to it," Lily mumbled.

"Well, what about school?" Amy asked. "Have you gotten to know any girls on dance team yet?"

Lily shrugged. "Not really. They seem like they're all such good friends. It's too weird trying to talk to anyone, so I just keep out of the way. I go to practice, then leave as soon as it ends. I don't even go to the locker rooms — I just change at home."

"Seriously?" Amy said. "Why?"

"Ugh," Lily moaned. "I can't sit in there and

listen to the girls chattering and making plans in the locker room without me! It's too depressing."

"Well, have you ever asked to tag along?" Amy pressed.

"Of course not! I'm the new girl," Lily reminded her. "I can't just force them to be my friends and invite me to things. And now we have the pep rally dance tomorrow. I know the routine, but I'm terrified. It's almost worse than not being on the dance team at all! And the team captain, Mia . . ."

"Not as good a captain as you were going to be?" Amy guessed.

"No, it's not that!" Lily protested. "Well . . . maybe a little. She's definitely one of the best dancers, but her attitude is the worst."

"Okay, so she's not the best captain ever. But no one else is nice?" Amy prodded.

"The coach is really good," Lily admitted. "The other girls are okay, I guess. There's this one girl, Jill . . . I sit in the courtyard for lunch sometimes, and I watch her and her friend Porter play hacky sack. It's better than sitting alone in the cafeteria."

"Don't worry, you'll have a bunch of friends soon. People just need to get to know you and see how fabulous you are!" Amy exclaimed.

"Enough about my depressing life," Lily said with a sigh. "What about you? How's the team? I miss you guys so much!"

"So I told you Coach held special tryouts to fill your spot, right? Well, Madison got it. I don't think you know her — she transferred from West this year. Anyway, she's awesome. She's helping me work on aerials."

"Really? That's . . . great," Lily said. She tried to ignore the empty feeling growing in her belly.

"Yeah, she's got a huge backyard and a basement all set up for practice," Amy explained. "I'm getting really good at my pop cartwheels. A bunch of us have just been hanging out there and doing extra practice on whatever lately."

Sounds like a lot of fun, Lily thought, her stomach in knots now. *Without me.*

"So, um, what song are you guys doing for your pep rally dance?" Lily asked, trying to change the subject.

She didn't feel like hearing more about Madison. It felt like all she was really hearing was that her old friends were moving on just fine without her.

Am I the only one still sad about this? Lily wondered, her heart sinking.

"Madison suggested we do that 'Shake the Room' song, and Coach went for it," Amy replied. "It's really fun. I bet Coach will post a video of the dance afterward."

"I'll watch for it," Lily said. Suddenly she didn't feel like being on the phone anymore. "Hey, my mom is calling me for dinner. I have to go. I'll text you tomorrow or something."

"Okay," Amy said. "Tell your mom I said hi!"

"Same," Lily said.

She turned off her phone and closed her eyes. Talking to Amy hadn't made her feel any happier. In fact, she felt worse. Her old team was doing fine without her. Maybe even better!

Lily felt like she didn't belong anywhere. She knew her old friends still loved her, but as much as she missed the Greenville dancers, they weren't her team anymore. The Panthers were.

Lily opened her eyes, and the room around her came into focus. The blank walls and stacks of boxes were so depressing. Living in limbo like this wasn't helping her.

It's time to stop acting like this move is just temporary. Wilmington is home now . . . whether I like it or not, she told herself. *Maybe if I make my room look more like home, it will start to feel that way too.*

Lily jumped off the bed and put on her favorite playlist. Then she went over to a pile of boxes and started opening them up, looking for her favorite posters and dance trophies.

After finding some old tack in her desk drawer, Lily began hanging things on the walls. A string of lights here, a poster there. Soon she was dancing as she worked; she didn't even notice until there was a knock at the door that made her jump.

"Come in!" Lily called, turning down the music.

Her mom walked in. A big smile spread across her face as she saw the new and improved room.

"Wow, someone finally decided to move in!" Mom joked. "It looks great. What happened?"

"Well, if I'm going to live here, I might as well make it nice," Lily said, shrugging. "Is dinner ready?"

"Soon," Mom replied. "You have time to work a little longer. I'll see you downstairs in ten?"

"Okay," Lily said. "Thanks, Mom."

It was funny, but just getting her things out of the boxes really was making her feel better. Lily started dancing again as she wound a scarf around one of the bedposts. Maybe tomorrow would be a better day.

CHAPTER 7

LEFT OUT

The next day was Friday, the day of the pep rally. In the locker room, Lily and her teammates were pulling on their uniforms.

"I'm so nervous," Jill said, sounding more excited than worried. "First performance! I hope I don't fall on my face."

"Nobody is falling," Alison said, poking her in the ribs. "We've totally got this!"

Mia put a foot up on the bench and bent low to stretch her long legs. "Are you ready to show some school spirit, Lily?" she asked.

Lily jumped a little when she heard her name. "What? Yes. I mean, yes! I'm full of spirit. Go, Panthers!" she said loudly.

And as she said it, Lily realized she really was ready to try. If she was ever going to feel like a Panther, now was the time to start.

"Go, Panthers!" all the girls shouted.

Coach Smith walked in right as the team finished their cheer. "That's the spirit," she said. "Keep it up out there, and you'll do great!"

Five minutes later, Lily was lined up with the rest of team at the gym door. On cue, Coach Smith pulled the door open, and they ran through.

The team rushed into the center of the gym. The bleachers were packed full of students and teachers. Everyone burst into wild cheering when they saw the dancers appear.

There was no time for nerves now. Lily and her teammates got into formation, waiting for the music to start.

Lily closed her eyes, and let the energy of the crowd take hold. This was her school now. This was her team. The first beats pounded out of the loudspeakers, and Lily let it move her body. She didn't think — she danced.

Left fist, right fist, shimmy, clap! Chasse left, jump. The moves that had felt slow and awkward before were finally flowing through her. *Kick, kick, spin, clap.*

Lily felt a smile appearing on her face, all by itself. It felt good to be moving as part of a team again.

The music was building to the climax. Lily took a deep breath as she marched forward to line up with Mia for the final move.

Lily spun to the right and then back-flipped to the left. Mia mirrored her movements, back-flipping to the right.

Lily felt the familiar rush as she glided through the air for a split second. Her feet hit the floor. She flung her arms high into the air, keeping her fingers perfectly pointed.

The crowd's cheering turned to a roar. Several students stood up, clapping loudly and whistling.

Lily grinned as relief flooded her. She'd nailed it!

* * *

In the locker room afterward, everyone was jumping around in celebration.

"See, I told you nobody was going to fall!" Alison said, laughing.

"I almost did on that layout," Nora admitted.

"No way," Emily argued. "You stuck it. I saw you."

"Wonderful work, Panthers!" Coach Smith said. "Just listen to that crowd. You did that."

The roars and stomps of applause at the end of the performance had been deafening. Lily had to admit that it felt pretty amazing to be a part of it.

"It wasn't just your steps," Coach said. "It was your spirit. Every one of you had such great energy tonight. If we can keep that up, this team is going to the state competitions for sure!"

"Go, Panthers!" the team cried.

"That ice cream tonight is going to taste soooo good!" Hannah exclaimed, pulling on her shoes.

"I'm getting two scoops," Mia said. "I totally earned it with that backflip."

Confused, Lily looked up from her bag. Had someone brought ice cream for the team?

"I'm going to be late because we have to take my brother to soccer, but I'll be there," Alison said.

"Hey, Hannah, can you give me a ride?" Nora chimed in.

"Yeah, no problem," Hannah said. "We're picking Jill up too."

Lily's excitement collapsed as she realized they were talking about a celebration she hadn't been invited to. She wondered if anyone would notice and invite her, but everyone seemed busy with dressing and making plans.

She briefly thought about what Amy had told her — maybe she should just ask to go along.

But what if they say no? Lily thought. *Besides, if they wanted me to come, they would've asked.*

Lily pulled on her clothes as quickly as she could, suddenly feeling self-conscious. Clearly she wasn't a part of the team after all. "Great job, guys," she said, trying to sound casual as she hurried out the door. "See you tomorrow."

"Aren't you coming to the football game tonight?" Jill called after her, but the door had already closed.

* * *

Mom was waiting at the curb. Lily tossed her gym bag in the back of the car and hopped inside.

"So . . . how did it go?" her mom asked as Lily buckled up.

"Good," Lily replied. She was quiet for a moment. "Really good. I danced like I haven't danced since camp. Mia and I nailed the backflip."

Mom leaned over and squeezed her tight. "That's so awesome, Lily! I knew you could do it. Are you going to the game tonight?"

"Nah," Lily said quickly. "We aren't performing, and Coach said we didn't have to go." She didn't feel like explaining that the rest of the team was going out to celebrate without her.

The car was quiet for a few minutes, then Mom spoke up. "Hey, I know. Why don't we go out for dinner tonight?" she suggested. "You've earned a treat. What are you in the mood for?"

"Tacos," Lily replied. "I want tacos." Despite the sadness she felt at being left out, she realized she was starving.

"Well, you're in luck. I heard about a great place downtown," Mom said. "Let's go get your dad, and we'll make an evening of it."

"Sounds good," Lily said quietly. If she didn't have any friends, at least she had her family.

CHAPTER 8

FACING THE TRUTH

At practice on Monday, Coach Smith opened with an announcement. "I have big news, everyone!" she said. "The downtown business association is putting on a big Fall Festival parade, and the Panthers have been invited to perform!"

The team cheered. Lily felt a thrill of excitement. She loved performing in front of big crowds.

"This will be different from our normal routines," Coach continued. "Instead of staying in the middle of a field or gym, the dance will have to constantly move forward along a two-mile parade route. You'll need to work hard to keep up your energy and concentration for the long performance." She handed out papers with the routine for the girls to start memorizing at home.

Lily quickly scanned the sheets. They would be lined up in three rows. Her heart fluttered when she saw that she was in the front. She would be on the left, Mia in center, and Jill on the right.

The girls warmed up quickly with some basic stretching. Then everyone gathered around Coach Smith, eager to start learning the new routine.

The team would make a few formations and a couple of line switches throughout the routine. But most of the dance would be performed in the three rows to help keep it organized and in time with the rest of the parade.

"Let's start with the first eight-count," Coach said. "Watch me, then we'll try it all together."

Coach punched her fist into the air, then spun into a dipping cross step. She finished by marching forward for a few beats, arms swinging in a big arc from left to right.

"Okay," she said, "let's get into position and see how we do."

Lily took her place in the front row with Mia and Jill. The rest of the team got in formation, and they practiced the eight-count over and over. The hardest part was making sure that everyone moved forward the same amount at the same speed. If they didn't, they'd get too bunched up or too spread out.

Once the team was moving forward in unison, Coach added the next eight-count, then the next. The third section had a full pirouette that rippled back along the lines of dancers, one row per beat. After the girls spun, they would bend low. Then they'd march in a crouch to allow the dancers pirouetting behind them to come into view.

As Lily got low to the ground after her spin, her steps wobbled slightly. Marching in a crouch felt awkward. She could see Jill looking shaky too. The team was also struggling to get the timing just right on the wave pattern.

After a few more run-throughs, Coach clapped her hands. "Good start, Panthers," she said. "We'll keep rehearsing this in practice, but you'll all need to work at home to get the routine ready in time. It's going to be hard, but I know we can pull it off. Are you up to the challenge?"

"Yes!" the team shouted.

Lily was excited about this new twist to the normal performance. She didn't mind hard work, not when it came to dance! Maybe she could finally show the Panthers what she was really made of.

* * *

At lunch the next day, Lily went out to the courtyard and sat on the wall as usual. She watched Jill and Porter and a couple of other kids kicking the hacky sack around.

As soon as Jill spotted her, she gave up her spot in the circle and came bounding over. "Hey, have you looked at the parade routine yet?" she asked. "I tried to run through it last night, and there are a few places I could really use some help. Would you want to work on it together after school?"

Lily was surprised. "Really? I mean . . . sure. That would be great. You can come over to my house whenever you want."

Jill looked relieved. "Great, thanks!" she said. "I'll find you at your locker after school." With that, she hopped off the wall and went back to the game.

* * *

Later that afternoon, Jill sat on Lily's bed and looked around. "I like your room," she said. "I have to share with my little sister, so mine still has a lot of baby stuff. This is great. Look at all those trophies!"

"It must be nice to have a sister, though," Lily said. "It's just me and my parents. It can get kind of boring and lonely sometimes. Actually a lot of the time, now that we moved."

"I guess you must miss your old friends?" Jill asked quietly.

"Yeah, I miss them," Lily admitted. "Plus . . . it's been really hard making friends here."

Jill crossed her arms. "But you have the team!"

"Yeah . . . I guess," Lily said carefully. "I mean, I'm really happy to be on the Panthers, but it's not like I know anyone that well. We don't exactly get together outside of school or anything." She smiled a little. "Until now."

"I didn't . . ." Jill trailed off. "You didn't really seem like you wanted to be friends. You never talk to anybody unless you have to. And you always run away at the end of practice. I think we were all a little scared to talk to you, honestly. You didn't even come celebrate with us after the pep rally."

Lily was shocked. *Have I completely misread my new teammates?* she wondered. *I know I've been kind of shy and sad lately. Has that been coming across as rude and cold?*

Lily was silent for a minute, gathering her thoughts. "I can't believe I made you guys think I didn't want to be friends," she said. "It seemed like you all had such a great bond after camp and all . . . I didn't think there was room for me."

"Are you kidding?" Jill exclaimed. "There's always room. We're totally excited to have you around! Come on. You've only been here a few weeks, and you're already one of the stars of the show."

"You are too!" Lily said, laughing.

"Don't remind me!" Jill cried, pulling a pillow over her face and falling back on the bed.

Lily grabbed the pillow and tossed it into a corner. "No! We're doing this! Let's go in the yard, where there's room. We're going to make this town love the Panthers!"

CHAPTER 9

BACK IN THE GROOVE

After Jill left, Lily ran back to her room. She logged onto her computer and immediately started messaging Amy.

Lily: OMG I am so dumb. All the dance girls thought I hated them!

Amy: What? How?

Lily: Jill came over to practice and told me. She said I never talk to anyone and that I run away after practice, which is true. How do I fix this with the rest of the team? I'm such a dork.

Amy: You are not! You can totally fix this. Why don't you have a party and invite everyone?

Lily: Yikes. Do you think anyone would come?

Amy: Stop it! You're doing it again.

Lily: Ugh, you're right! Okay, a party. I have to start planning.

Amy: That's the spirit! :) Can't wait to hear how it goes.

Lily decided to invite her new teammates over the following Saturday. The weather was supposed to be beautiful, so they would be able to hang out and play games in the backyard. Lily's mom was so happy that she was finally making friends, she agreed to the party right away. Now all that was left to do was invite her new teammates.

On Tuesday, Lily didn't go home right after practice. Instead, she went into the locker room with all the other girls. Lily waited nervously for a break in the conversation. As Emily finished a long speech about how she was never going to figure out a back handspring, Lily finally broke in.

"So I was thinking about having a party on Saturday. For the team. If you guys want to come over . . ." Lily trailed off as everyone turned to look at her. Her stomach fluttered in the silence.

But Jill spoke up happily. "Awesome! What time?" she said. Then the other girls started chiming in.

"Hey, that's great! Where do you live?" Emily asked.

"Oh," Lily said. "Um, it's at two o'clock, and I can write down my address."

"Can I get a ride?" Hannah was asking Alison.

"Yeah, text me . . ."

Lily was flooded with relief. It was actually working!

* * *

The girls started arriving a little after two
o'clock on Saturday. Lily hovered anxiously near
the door to greet each guest. But her nerves began
to melt away as the backyard filled with happy
laughter.

By the time Jill arrived with Emily, Lily had
given up her post by the door and headed out
back. Her teammates filled the yard. Some chatted
by the snack table. Others danced to the music that
was playing. A few climbed on the tire swing that
hung from a giant oak tree.

"Great party, Lily!" Jill exclaimed, coming over
to her.

"Thanks!" Lily said. She gave a big grin. "It feels
really good to be hanging out with everyone."

Lily and Jill walked over to the swing, and
they watched as Nora and Alison balanced on

opposite sides of the big tire. Soon the two began leaning back and forth in unison, making it swing crazily.

Lily gave the tire a push when it swung near her, adding a spin. Nora shrieked with laughter. Soon all the other girls started shouting for a turn.

It took them all a while to notice that Mia had come in through the back gate. She was watching everyone with a frown on her face. Lily was the first to spot her.

"Hey, Mia!" she said, swallowing her nerves and walking over. Mia was a teammate too, after all. "Want a snack or anything?"

"I'm good," Mia said, barely glancing at the table of food.

Jill hopped off the tire swing. "Hey, Mia, want a turn on this thing?" she called. "It's ridiculous, but it's fun."

Mia shrugged and walked over. Seeming bored, she climbed on the tire swing. She stood in the inner ring, holding onto the rope. "Anyone going to push?" she asked.

Hannah stepped forward and gave the tire a shove. As it swung back and forth in a wide arc, Mia pulled herself up to sit on the top of the tire, legs around the rope. She hooked her feet inside the rim of the tire and slowly leaned back until her long hair brushed the grass.

"Ooooh," Hannah said, impressed.

All eyes were on Mia now. She let her arms fall out to the sides like a tightrope walker. As she began to sit up, one of her feet suddenly slipped from its grip inside the tire. Her legs flew up in the air, and she tumbled from the top of the swing.

Mia landed flat on her back in the grass with a loud "Oof!" There was a long moment of total silence.

Lily ran forward. She bent next to Mia and offered her a hand. "Mia, are you okay?" she asked.

Mia lay still for a few moments, just looking at her. She slowly took Lily's hand and sat up. "Fine," Mia whispered hoarsely. Her face was red, and she was taking shaky breaths.

The other girls started to gather around, but Lily waved them back. "She's okay, just give her a little room," she said. "She needs to catch her breath."

Mia wouldn't look at anyone. She just sat on the ground. Lily sat with her, a gentle arm around her shoulders.

Finally, Mia shrugged her off. Lily looked at her flushed face, then at the circle of girls standing around, staring.

"Do you know I did that once at a school picnic?" Lily announced. Mia looked at her.

So did everyone else. "In front of a guy I liked? I was trying to impress him with my new back walkover skills. But the ground was muddy. I slipped and knocked the breath right out of myself. It was horrible. Plus I was covered in mud."

A small smile crept onto Mia's face. "What a nerd," she said softly.

"Yeah, a total nerd. I couldn't even look at him after that," Lily added, smiling back.

Jill spoke up. "I kicked a hacky sack into my own eye last week," she offered.

"I broke my elbow dancing at a wedding," Alison said. "All my cousins laughed at me."

Mia's face began to go back to its usual color as most of the team started wandering off toward the snack table. Each girl was now trying to tell the most embarrassing story. Mia finally stood, and Lily followed.

"That was nice of you," Mia said, sounding surprised. "You didn't have to do that."

Lily shrugged. "We're a team, right?"

"Yeah, I guess we are," Mia agreed. "Thanks, teammate."

"Anytime, Captain," Lily replied.

CHAPTER 10

FLOURISH

A week later, when the Panthers filed into the locker room after practice, they were still talking about Lily's party. And Lily chatted right along with them. Practices had been tough as they perfected the parade routine, but she was finally feeling truly in sync with her team.

Now it was time for the big Fall Festival parade. The team was in the staging area at the center of town, ready to perform. The place was a mess of people and sound. Brass band music blared. Crowds swirled. Lily and her teammates huddled together near the edge of the big parking lot, waiting for instructions.

"I can't believe this!" Lily exclaimed. She couldn't decide if she was more nervous or excited. This wasn't a competition, but it was definitely the most public event in which she'd ever performed.

"The whole town has to be in this parking lot. Who will watch the parade?" Emily joked.

Finally, the Panthers were called to line up. The dancers followed Coach Smith over to the starting area, then arranged themselves into their three lines.

"I'll be riding in the cart behind you with the speakers," Coach reminded the team. She had to shout to be heard over the crowd. "We'll march in line until we reach the beginning of the route, on the street. Then I'll start the music. Listen for that intro, watch your leaders for the pace, and stay focused. And most importantly . . ."

"Have fun!" the team finished.

Coach smiled. "See, you've got this," she said. Then she climbed into the cart to make sure everything was ready to go.

A few minutes later, a loud whistle blew, and the procession began to slowly make its way into the street. Lily and her teammates were in the middle of the line, but they could hear loud cheering from the crowds as the parade started. The dancers shook their bodies out, throwing in some last-minute stretches.

Lily folded herself in half and grasped her ankles, feeling her hamstrings stretch. *No stiffness allowed today,* she thought. *This is it!*

As they moved forward with the parade, the sidewalk came into view. Then they were in the street. Once the last girls were out of the parking lot, the music began. It was showtime.

One, two, three, punch! Spin, step, spin, step.
Lily felt the music swelling above the noise of the crowd. People cheered all along both sides of the street as the team moved confidently with the beat.

On her left, Mia was dancing with big, strong gestures. Beyond the team captain, Jill was performing with a sassy snap in her steps. And behind them was the rest of the team.

My team, Lily thought. A big smile crept across her face as she realized that there was nowhere else she would rather be. She whirled in a perfect pirouette, then crouched low.

Lily, Mia, and Jill marched behind a large trailer carrying a display covered in giant papier–mâché flowers and plants. They all kept an eye on the display as they went forward. It was their job to control the team's pace. They needed to make sure to keep a wide stretch of space between their group and the end of the trailer.

With the pirouette wave done, the girls did a forward roll back to their feet. They stretched their arms into high Vs, then snapped them down. As they danced forward along the route, their lines crossed once, then twice. They ended back in the original formation with Mia in the center.

Lily took a deep breath — now for the showstopper.

As the team neared the platform where the bleachers for the most important spectators stood, Lily spun to the center and caught Jill's eye. Jill gave a slight nod. They spun to the outside in unison, then back to face each other on either side of Mia.

The team danced for a moment in place behind them, while Jill and Lily jazz-walked behind Mia. They kneeled so that their raised knees touched.

Mia twirled around, facing her two teammates. Lily braced herself as Mia lifted her hands up and fell forward. The team captain planted her palms firmly on Lily's and Jill's thighs and lifted her body into a perfect handstand.

Lily supported Mia by placing one hand on the girl's hip. The other hand she held out high to the side. Jill mirrored her.

The three girls held the pose for a moment, then Mia kicked down to the ground. She launched straight into a back handspring, sticking her landing with a flourish. At the same time, Jill and Lily crossed behind her with a couple of kickovers. They each came to rest in front of the other's line. The team fell in line behind them again, marching on to the sound of wild cheering.

Lily breathed hard as they continued forward. She glanced over to Mia. The two exchanged a small smile before focusing their eyes back to the front.

As the Panthers passed the bleachers, something caught Lily's eye. Someone in a bright pink jacket was jumping around and shouting even more loudly than the rest of the crowd. There, along with her parents, was Amy!

Lily beamed at her old friend. Her heart swelled at the sight of that familiar face. Before she had to look away, she saw Amy's mom wave and wink.

A new burst of energy moved Lily as she danced down the street with the Panthers. She couldn't believe Amy had surprised her! And now that she was here, Lily couldn't wait to show her friend around Wilmington. There was so much that she wanted to share — the great taco place downtown, her cool room, the amazing tire swing in her backyard . . . but most importantly, her new team.

ABOUT the AUTHOR

Leigh McDonald loves books! Whether she is writing them, reading them, editing them, or designing their covers, books are what she does best. Leigh has written several books in the successful Jake Maddox Girl Sport Stories series, including *Dance Team Dilemma* and *Volleyball Victory.* She lives in a colorful bungalow in Tucson, Arizona, with her husband, Porter, her two daughters, Adair and Faye, and two big, crazy dogs, Roscoe and Rosie.

GLOSSARY

confidence (KON-fi-duhns) — the belief in your own abilities and knowing that you can do something

flourish (FLUR-ish) — a fancy way of doing something to add interest and drama; to grow or be successful

formation (for-MAY-shuhn) — the way in which members of a group are arranged; dance formations often make a certain shape or design

intruder (in-TROO-der) — a person who is uninvited or not wanted

limbo (LIM-boh) — the state of being in between two things

routine (roo-TEEN) — a series of planned movements that make up a performance

self-conscious (SELF-KON-shuss) — nervous and embarrassed by what other people might be thinking about you

synchronized (SING-kruh-nizd) — done at the same time and speed

temporary (TEM-puh-rair-ee) — lasting for only a short time

DISCUSSION QUESTIONS

1. In your own words, describe some of the reasons why Lily was unhappy at her new school. Talk about what in the story made you think that.

2. Moving can be difficult. Have you ever moved or had a friend move away? Discuss your experience or what you think it would be like.

3. How does Lily feel at the end of the story? Why? Talk about how her attitude changed throughout the story, and be sure to use examples from the text to support your answers.

WRITING PROMPTS

1. Jill told Lily that the other girls on the team thought Lily didn't want to be friends. Write a few paragraphs from the perspective of one of the other dancers, like Jill or Mia, and show how she felt about Lily joining the team.

2. Lily took charge and threw a get-together for her teammates. Make a list of ways you would make new friends if you moved.

3. Write a paragraph about what kind of team captain you think Lily would be. How would she act? How would she treat her teammates? Point to specific examples in the story to support your reasoning.

MORE ABOUT
DANCE TEAMS

The modern dance team developed from **pep squads**. In the 1920s, schools and colleges started forming pep squads to inspire school spirit. At first, the groups borrowed many of their moves from **marching bands** and **military drills**. Over time, the groups combined more and more popular music and dance with the military exactness of their formations.

In 1940, **Gussie Nell Davis** organized the **Kilgore College Rangerettes**. The drill team became famous for performing at football games and other events, popularizing drill and dance teams.

Dr. Kay Teer Crawford is often called the "mother of drill team." In 1967, she organized **Miss Dance Drill Team USA** — the first national competition for dance teams, drill teams, and dance studios. The competition was a big success and still runs to this day.

THE FUN DOESN'T
STOP HERE!

FIND MORE AT:
CAPSTONEKIDS.COM

Authors and Illustrators | Videos and Contests
Games and Puzzles | Heroes and Villains

Find cool websites and
more books like this one at
www.facthound.com
Just type in the Book ID:
9781496536747
and you're ready to go!

Dance is fun, but it also has many **health benefits.** Dancing regularly can boost memory, improve flexibility, reduce stress, strengthen your heart, lessen depression, improve balance, and increase energy. Dancers are **athletes!**

In competitions, dance teams are judged on many criteria, such as **form, team unison, showmanship, precision** of motions, **jumps, leaps, turns, choreography,** and **enthusiasm.** Team spirit is also important!

There are many types of dance teams, but all of them focus on exact, **synchronized motions** and **technical dance skills.** Another key feature of a dance team routine is the ability to change **formations** very smoothly.

Routines can draw from many **styles** of dancing. **Hip-hop, lyrical,** and **kickline** dances are very common, but routines can even incorporate styles like disco, rock and roll, and gospel. Skills like **tumbling** and **cheer** are also very important.